GW00865838

EZZIE'S EMERALD

EZZIE'S EMERALD

by

KATHLEEN McDONNELL

Illustrated by Sally J.K. Davies

SECOND
STORY
Press

For my good friends Martha Farquhar-McDonnell,
Elizabeth Filyer-Dewdney and Carla Rose Anderson

CANADIAN CATALOGUING IN PUBLICATION DATA

McDonnell, Kathleen, 1947-
Ezzie's emerald

ISBN 0-929005-13-9

I. Title.

PS8575.D66E98 1990 jC813'.54 C90-095067-6
P27.M33Ez 1990

Second Story Press gratefully acknowledges
the assistance of the Ontario Arts Council

Copyright © Kathleen McDonnell 1990

Printed and Bound in Canada

Published by
SECOND STORY PRESS
760 Bathurst Street
Toronto Canada M5S 2R6

CONTENTS

I

IN HECK

THAT MORNING Ezzie had a snarl in her hair that wouldn't come out.

"Stop dawdling in front of that mirror, Esme."

"I've got a snarl," said Ezzie.

"If you wore your hair shorter, you wouldn't get so many snarls," said her mother.

"I don't want short hair," said Ezzie, thinking of Shay, one of the Grade 7 girls at school, who had long, straight hair. She was always tossing her head back, trying to keep her hair out of her eyes. A couple of times

Ezzie stood in front of the mirror, trying to toss her own hair back in the same way. But she couldn't quite get the motion right.

Her mother gathered Ezzie's hair into a ponytail.

"Could you do a French braid?" Ezzie implored her.

"No time, honey. I'm running late. Help Anna with her clothes, will you? While I get breakfast?"

Ezzie went into the bedroom. Her four-year-old sister Anna had taken a turtleneck out of the drawer and started to pull it over her head.

"Oh no! It's the headless monster again!" cried Ezzie, seeing Anna with the turtleneck stuck halfway over her head.

Anna started to giggle and ran out of the room. Ezzie chased her into the kitchen, laughing too.

Anna couldn't see where she was going, and raced right into her mother, almost knocking the bowls of cereal out of her hands.

"For God's sake, Esme!" said her

mother. "I ask you to help me and you act like a two-year-old."

Ezzie helped Anna finish dressing, and then the three of them sat down to breakfast.

"Mom, can we call Dad tonight?"

"I hoped he would have phoned you two by now," said her mother. "You haven't heard from him since Christmas."

"Yeah, he forgot Valentine's Day!" Anna piped up.

"He's been busy with the new baby, you dork," Ezzie shot back. "Hasn't he, Mom?"

"I'm sure that's true, honey."

"So could I?"

"It's pretty expensive to phone out west. We'll see after dinner, okay?"

As they were getting ready to leave, Ezzie pulled her jean jacket off the hook where it had been hanging since the fall.

"Honey, wear your winter jacket."

"No! It was warm yesterday," said Ezzie. "I got all sweaty."

"But it's still too cold for a jean jacket."

"No it isn't!" Ezzie was insistent.

"I haven't got time to argue with you," her mother sighed.

"Oops!" Ezzie suddenly bolted toward the bedroom. "Forgot my sticker book."

"Honey, we're late!"

"But I need it," Ezzie called from her bedroom. "Me and Mai and Sarah are trading stickers at lunch. Go on without me. It's nice out. I'll walk."

"Okay, hon. Don't forget your knapsack here by the door!"

A few minutes later Ezzie came out of the house, trying to stuff the sticker book into her knapsack without mashing her lunch bag. Her mom and Anna were just pulling away in the car, and Ezzie waved to them. She dropped Anna off at the day care on her way to work every day. But Ezzie's school was only three blocks away, with no busy streets to cross. Just this year she had started walking to school on her own.

Ezzie started out, enjoying the unusually mild, bright March morning. Near the top of Margaret Street, she jumped through the hopscotch she and Angela DiCecco had drawn yesterday. Ezzie went to Angie's house most days after school, until her mom got home from work.

Sometimes Angie followed her around at school, wanting to play. But Ezzie was too embarassed for her friends to see her playing with a little Grade 1 squirt like Angela.

She saw Mrs. DiCecco come out of her house pushing her baby, Nina, in the stroller, and waved to them. A couple of houses down from the DiCecco's was the part of the walk she hated — the house with the BE-WARE OF DOG sign. Most mornings she tried walking past it very quietly, but, as usual, it didn't work. The dog saw her and followed her along the length of the fence, snarling and barking and pulling on the long rope tied to its collar.

Sometimes in the morning she'd see

the dog's owner leaving for work, shutting the gate behind him. Once, when the dog started barking at her, the man yelled "Shut up, you!" and kicked the dog so hard that it made Ezzie wince. Then the dog skulked off into a corner of the yard, whimpering.

"Somebody's going to get hurt if that dog ever gets loose," her mother often said.

She continued on up the block, the dog's barks ringing after her. She noticed a familiar figure coming out of the house next to the variety store.

"Hey Josh!" she called out. "Wait up!"

He turned and waved, stopping at the edge of the sidewalk to wait for her. All her other friends were girls now, but Josh was her old buddy. The two of them had played together since they were babies — their moms were best friends.

"Hi," Josh called. "You walking today?"

"Felt like it," said Ezzie, as she got up close. "Hey, what's that?" she said, pointing to something sticking out of the back of Josh's knapsack. It was a large white feather with a black tip.

"An eagle feather," said Josh, taking it out of the pack and handing it to her. "My dad got it for me."

Their class was doing bird projects for natural science. Josh's was on the bald eagle. Ezzie was doing hers on the ruby-throated hummingbird.

Ezzie ran her fingers lightly along the feather's delicate hairs, thinking about her own father, now living over a thousand miles away, with a new wife and baby. "Neat," she said as she handed it back to Josh.

"Know what I found out? In the old days they used to use feathers for pens."

"No kidding," said Ezzie. "Did you know that a hummingbird beats its wings over thirty-five hundred times a minute?"

"Wow!" said Josh.

They walked the rest of the way together, talking about their projects. But as they approached the playground they separated, walking through the gate almost as if they didn't know one another. Inside the playground, Josh joined the group of boys gathered by the fence. Ezzie ran to the large circle of girls in the centre of the yard.

Her best friends, Sarah and Mai, were there, along with a bunch of other Grade 3 girls.

"Did you hear?" Sarah said as she came up to them. "Ryan's not in school today. He's got cooties."

"Aw, too bad!" Ezzie crowed. The girls all laughed. Ryan Coombs was one of the jerkiest boys in the school. He was always doing gross things, like making himself belch and laughing about it.

"Say the spell right away!" Mai yelled at Ezzie. "His hook's right near yours!"

Ezzie pulled back her jacket sleeve, closed her eyes, and made a circular motion on her bare arm, saying as she did it: "Circle, circle, dot, dot. Now I got my cooties shot."

"Whew! Now you're safe," said Sarah.

There was a commotion nearby. One of the other girls, Lesley, had gotten into a shouting match with Jake, one of Ryan's pals. Ezzie and her friends weren't crazy about Ryan, but they couldn't stand Jake. He was always picking on people for no good reason.

"Bet you got the cooties, too!" Lesley yelled at him.

"I'd rather have cooties than stink-breath like you!" Jake retorted.

Mai and some of the other girls joined in with Lesley's taunts, but Ezzie hung back from the group. She didn't want to call Jake's attention to herself. Not if she could avoid it.

Lesley and Jake finally got tired of their argument. Sarah called out, "Let's play wild ponies!" And the girls quickly formed a herd, neighing and bucking at each other as they ran around the playground. Ezzie watched them from the fence, until Mai called over to her, "Come on, Stardust!" Stardust was the name Ezzie used when they played ponies. After a minute she joined in, laughing and running around with the others. Then it started — again — just like a million times before.

"Hippo! Hippo!" Jake called out as she ran past. "Fat hippo, hippo!"

Some other boys started to laugh. Ezzie's face burned. But she pretended not to hear them, and kept on running.

That was what her mother had said to do. "Just ignore him, honey. Pretend you don't even hear him. Jake will get tired of it if he can't get a rise out of you."

At first Ezzie had tried playing songs in her head to drown him out. But Jake kept it up, day after day. She didn't talk to her mother about it again. She didn't want to bother her. Anyway, she thought, what was the point? Nothing would make him stop. Jake was a weasel, a slime, a rotten creep.

A flush of anger came over Ezzie. Why should she care what he did? She resolved that from now on she just wasn't going to let him bother her any more, not the least little bit. She wouldn't hear him, wouldn't look at him. It would be like he didn't even exist.

For a moment she felt better, lighter, sure that she could calm the churning feeling

in her stomach. Then she heard some loud, snorting noises. In spite of herself, she looked over in Jake's direction. He had his belly stuck out in front of him, mocking the way she ran. One of the younger boys, Pedro, started calling out "Hippo! Hippo!" A bunch of the other boys stood around watching them and laughing. Ezzie suddenly felt stung, like someone had slapped her across the face. On the edge of the group stood Josh, laughing along with the rest of them.

The bell rang, and swarms of kids began streaming through the doors of the school. Ezzie found herself standing behind Pedro, looking down on his dark, curly hair. She gave him a quick, hard punch on the back of the head. Pedro yowled in pain, and Ezzie heard a sharp, familiar voice behind her.

"I saw that, Esme Phelan!"

Ezzie felt her stomach sink. It would have to be one of Ms. Francis' supervision days. Why didn't she think to look around first, to make sure nobody would see her?

Ms. Francis was striding toward her.

"What's the meaning of this, Esme?"

"I was only fooling around, Ms. Francis, I didn't mean to hurt him..."

"You whacked that boy hard enough to knock him over. He's barely half your size."

"But Ms. Francis, he was – "

"No excuses, Esme. You know the rules. I'm very disappointed in you. Take yourself straight to the principal's office."

Ms. Francis turned and walked away with Pedro, who was rubbing the back of his head and whimpering.

Little brat, thought Ezzie. He's not hurt that bad, he's just playing up like he is. Her eyes started to blur with tears. It made her feel awful, being in heck with Ms. Francis. She ran toward the side entrance so that no one would see her cry.

2

TIMES FIVE
TROUBLE

A BUNCH OF GIRLS buzzed around Ezzie as she entered the classroom.

"C'mon. What'd Mr. Carpenter say to you? Tell, tell."

"Nothing," Ezzie told them. "He wasn't there. He's at a meeting downtown."

"You're lucky!" said Lisa. "He lectured me for ten minutes." Last week Lisa had to go down to the principal's office because she passed around a note with a swear word on it.

"Ladies," said Ms. Francis, "find your places on the carpet, please." The group around Ezzie broke up. She wondered if Ms. Francis would say she had to go back down to the office later. But the teacher was rifling through some papers on her desk and didn't look up as Ezzie walked past.

Ezzie looked for a place to sit down. Josh and several other boys hung out around the edge of the carpet, kicking and wrestling. The girls clustered together, positioning themselves so they could do Crisscross Applesauce on each other's backs. As usual, several girls bickered over who would get to sit with Melodie, who was so cute and tiny. Ezzie was glad to see Mai and Sarah make room for her between them.

"I can't hear a pin drop yet," said Ms. Francis. The din of the girls' chatter quickly died down. A couple of the boys kept on wrestling. The teacher fixed a silent, stony gaze on them until they scrambled apart.

"Miss Menkes will be reading to you this morning," said Ms. Francis. "I'm sure you will be the soul of courtesy, and give her your undivided attention while I'm out of the room."

Ms. Francis handed the book to Miss Menkes and left the room. Miss Menkes was a student teacher, and this was only her second day in Ms. Francis' room. On the playground yesterday, Ezzie and her friends had engaged in a fierce debate about Miss Menkes.

"Her thighs are fat!" Lisa stated firmly.

"Yeah, they're gross," agreed Tamara. Some of the other girls laughed.

"Just 'cause they're not toothpicks, like yours." said Sarah. "I like her. She has a really nice face."

"Yeah, right," Lisa retorted. "That's what you're supposed to say about a fat lady." And she recited in a mocking, singsong voice: "But she has such a pretty face!"

Ezzie felt herself shrink inside. That was exactly what her mother had said, when she tried putting her on that diet: "You have a pretty face, Esme. You'd look so nice if you could only lose a bit of that weight."

But Miss Menkes had begun reading, and Ezzie's attention turned back to the sound of the student teacher's voice.

The story was about a boy who had a magic peach pit. It changed into an emerald whenever it was in his hands, but turned back into a peach pit when anyone else held it. It got Ezzie thinking about her own emerald, the one her Aunt Rue had given her on her last birthday.

She still wondered what had happened to it. They'd turned the whole house upside down looking for it. Finally, her mom blew up and told Ezzie it was her responsibility to keep track of her own things. That night she'd cried herself to sleep. The emerald was one of the most special presents she'd ever gotten. How could she be so stupid, to go and lose it like that?

Ms. Francis came back into the room. She began passing out a sheet of paper — with a border of numbers and a blank box at the top — onto each student's desk. Just as Miss Menkes was finished Chapter 2, Ms. Francis called out: "Minute Math!"

Ezzie shot like a rocket back to her desk.

Minute Math was a fantastic game Ms. Francis had taught the class. To start the quiz, the teacher called out a number, and either "plus" or "times." They would write the number in a box, then add it to, or multiply it by, as many of the numbers around the edge as they could in one minute. All week her name had been second after Lisa's at the top of the chart on the bulletin board. If she did well in Minute Math today, she had a good chance of moving up to first place!

Everyone sat with their pencils poised. As soon as Ms. Francis called out the number the pencils began to fly, and they furiously recorded their answers in the boxes.

In what seemed to Ezzie like a few seconds, Ms. Francis called out, "Time's up!" They all brought up their sheets and placed them on her desk. Ezzie was a bit surprised to see how many kids had finished more of their sheet than she had. After all, the 5 times' table wasn't that easy. They hadn't even done it before in Minute Math. As she placed her sheet in the bin, she saw a "plus" sign next to the 5 in the centre of Lisa's sheet.

"Lisa," she said. "You did plus five." Ezzie was thrilled. Now she'd be moving up to first place for sure.

"So?" Lisa replied.

"We were supposed to do *times* five."

"Times five? You're cah-ray-zee!" said Lisa scornfully.

Ezzie walked back to the desk and looked at the pile of sheets. She saw plus 5 on the top one. She felt sick inside, and quickly flipped through the pile. Plus 5.

Plus 5. Plus 5.

The teacher looked up at her. "Is something the matter, Esme?"

"I think I made a mistake," Ezzie mumbled. Ms. Francis rifled through the pile and pulled out Ezzie's sheet, scanning quickly.

"I'm afraid you did, dear."

Ezzie turned away quickly and walked back to her desk. She looked the other way as she passed Lisa's desk, so she wouldn't have to see the disgusting ear-to-ear grin on her face.

3

STICKER
BUSINESS

IT WAS LUNCHTIME. Ezzie finished her sandwich in the lunchroom, then went outside carrying her sticker book and the big yellow apple her mother had packed. Ezzie liked apples, but she also wished she had a candy bar, or a pudding roll-up like Melodie's mom always sent.

Mai and Sarah came over clutching their sticker books. Ezzie made room for them on the steps, and the three girls began trading stickers in earnest.

They quickly flipped through their pages of regular, puffy, and fuzzy stickers. When they got to food stickers, Mai traded Sarah a milk shake for one of her fuzzy ducks. Ezzie turned to her shiny sticker page.

"You're lucky," Sarah told her. "You have the best shinies. Trade you these two stars for that big fish," she said.

"Okay, if you throw in that birthday cake, too," Ezzie replied.

Sarah paused. No use haggling with Ezzie. She was a good sticker trader.

"Okay," she finally said.

They moved on to their smelly stickers. Ezzie had her eye on one of Sarah's, a beautiful mermaid with scratch-and-sniff perfume, when Mai leaned over and whispered to Ezzie, "Do you have any umgla?"

It was their secret word for gum. You

had to be careful not to let on that you had gum on the playground, because all the other girls would come up to you begging for some, until you didn't have any left for yourself.

Ezzie remembered the pack she'd bought yesterday with the change from her milk money. What had she done with it?

"Be right back!" she said, and ran back into the building. Ms. Francis' room was right on the first floor. Ezzie went straight to her hook and reached into her knapsack. Still there. She pulled out the gum and raced back out to the playground.

When she got there, Mai and Sarah were having a giggling fit.

"Hey, what's so funny?" she asked, but they were both laughing too hard to answer.

Mai and Sarah did that sometimes — got silly together, and Ezzie wouldn't know what it was about. Usually she didn't let it bother her, but too many things had already gone wrong today. She definitely didn't feel like being left out.

"C'mon, what's the big joke?" she persisted.

Finally Mai struggled to form words through her giggles.

"We were wondering if you could get fart-smell into a sticker!"

"And give it to Jake!" Sarah finished, and they both doubled over in laughter again.

Ezzie started to giggle, too. But when Mai lunged for the pack of gum in her hand, Ezzie whipped it back out of reach.

"Don't grab!" she shouted, but the other two girls, still giggling, reached behind Ezzie's back, trying to grab the gum.

"Why don't you just advertise it over the loudspeaker?" Ezzie yelled, pulling away from them and sticking the gum in her pocket.

Sarah saw that Ezzie was serious, and abruptly stopped laughing. "Sor-ry!" she said sharply.

"Because of you guys the whole playground's going to know," said Ezzie. "Everybody's going to want some."

"They will not," said Sarah disdainfully, waving her arm toward a nearby cluster of kids. "Nobody's even paying any attention!"

Ezzie looked around, feeling a bit foolish. Sarah was right. Nobody was paying any attention to them.

Mai was still having trouble stifling her giggles. "We were only playing around, Ezzie," she managed to say.

Ezzie took the gum out of her pocket and offered some to both of them, a peace offering. They both took a stick.

"C'mon, let's trade stickers some more," said Mai, and the three of them settled back down on the steps. Ezzie scanned Sarah's smellies' page for the mermaid sticker, but it was gone.

"Hey!" she said, spying it in Mai's book. "Did you just trade for that?"

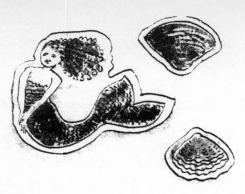

Mai nodded.

"I wanted that one," said Ezzie.

Sarah shrugged. "We didn't know."

"Trade you one of my best shinies," Ezzie said to Mai.

Mai considered for a moment, then finally shook her head. "I want to keep it for a while."

Ezzie slammed her book shut.

"No fair!"

"What's no fair?" Sarah demanded.

"I was just about to trade you for that!"

"So?"

"So I go to get us gum, and you guys do trades without me!"

"Ezzie!" Mai said in a loud whisper. "You forgot to use the secret word!"

"Don't care!" Ezzie shouted.

"I don't want to trade stickers any more," said Sarah, shutting her book and standing up.

"Neither do I!" retorted Ezzie. "At least not with you!"

"Come on, Mai. She's just in a bad mood 'cause she screwed up her Minute Math."

Ezzie watched them walk away.

"Why don't you go play with the kindergarten kids?" she shouted after them. "That's how old you act."

"Why don't you shut up?" Mai called out over her shoulder.

Ezzie shot up to her feet.

"I don't shut up, I grow up, but when I see your face I throw up! " she yelled at Mai, rushing the words together the way they always did.

But the minute the words were out she wished she could swallow them back. This was something you only said to your worst enemy, never to a friend, even if you were really mad at her.

Mai burst into tears and ran off.

"You can be so mean, Ezzie Phelan! I hate you!"

4

LOST AND
FOUND

WHEN THE BELL rang at 3:30 P. M. Ezzie grabbed her jacket and knapsack and hurried out the door. She decided to take the long way home, through the park in back of the school. That way she wouldn't see anybody and could be by herself.

As she crossed the small parking lot she started thinking about her dad. Mom was right. He should've called by now. She'd sent him that valentine and everything. Maybe he didn't get it. Maybe the address was wrong. But no, she remembered copying it down from the return address on the Christmas presents he'd sent. So he had gotten it. He just hadn't called. He was too busy with the new baby. What was the baby's name again? Charlotte. Charlotte Rose. A Christmas present — a new baby sister, he'd told Ezzie. Big deal. She already had a sister. She didn't *want* another one. Her eyes burned with tears. He should've phoned by now. He *should've.*

"Ez! Wait up!" It was Josh, calling from across the street. She pretended not to hear him, but he started racing after her.

"You going home?"

"None of your business!" she yelled irritably, not even looking back. Stupid jerk, she thought. Couldn't he tell she just wanted to be left alone?

"Sheesh!" Josh said. "What's with you?"

Ezzie whirled around to face him.

"I hate people who act like they're your friend and then laugh at you when they're with someone else!"

"Aw, come on — " he started to say,

38

but she cut him off.

"Go walk home with Jake and the rest of your big buddies!"

As she turned away, she noticed the eagle feather still sticking out of the top of his knapsack.

"I hope they laugh at your stupid feather!" she added, racing off so she wouldn't hear what he yelled back.

In a minute she was at the walkway leading into the park. Great, she thought. Now every single one of my friends is mad at me.

She felt like having something sweet, but she knew her lunch bag was empty. Then she remembered the gum she'd shared on the playground with Mai and Sarah. She shoved her hands into her pockets and felt around. There ought to be some left. Or hadn't Mai given the rest of it back to her? She couldn't remember.

She rifled around some more. Nothing. She went over to the bench by the fountain and started pulling things out of her pockets. A button and some wads of old Kleenex. A crumpled Mr. Big wrapper and some orange and-black striped cellophane left over from her Halloween candy. A note about a field trip she'd forgotten to give her mom last fall. An eraser. A dried-out piece of orange peel.

And stones. Always stones. "It's bad enough you keep all this other junk, Esme," her mother would say, going through her pockets. "But these rocks!"

She put everything but the eraser and the button and the stones in a nearby garbage bin. She put the other things back into her pocket, and tossed the stones onto the grass. But one small green one bounced back onto the pavement. She bent down to pick it up.

When she looked at it more closely, she could hardly believe what she saw. Hot wow! Her emerald! She'd found it!

None of the kids had believed her when she told them it was an emerald.

"Real emeralds are round and shiny!" said Lisa.

"No they're not!" Ezzie insisted. "Not when they first come out of the ground. My aunt got it in Peru. It's a *raw* emerald," she said emphatically.

Aunt Rue told her that the long form of her name in Spanish was Esmeralda, which meant emerald in Spanish. Ezzie hadn't known that before. Rue also said that emeralds had magic powers, that the stone would protect her and bring her good luck as long as she carried it with her. Ezzie didn't tell her mom about all that because she knew she'd say what she always said about Rue: "Pay no attention to my sister, she's a complete flake."

That was last November. After all she'd gone through about losing it, the emerald had been sitting right here in her pocket all this time!

Ezzie rolled the stone around in her palm. It was smaller than a dime, several tiny blue-green pillars clustered together, like a miniature kingdom. She thought of the Emerald City in *The Wizard of Oz*. It didn't gleam and glisten like the emeralds in that story. And was it really a magic stone? she wondered. It sure hadn't done her much good today. Anyway, she wasn't even sure she believed in magic any more. Sarah and Mai said it was okay to play at magic, but to really believe in it was just babyish.

Who was right, Mai and Sarah, or Aunt Rue? She didn't know. But something in her *wanted* to believe that the emerald was magic.

"I wish ... " The words ran through her mind.

She held back, feeling awkward, silly, like a little kid. But the feeling of wishing gripped her more fiercely and a whole stream of words began to flood into her mind.

"I wish Daddy would call. I wish Jake would leave me alone. I wish I could get out

of heck with Mai and Sarah and Josh. I wish I was beautiful and popular, like Shay or Melodie, and the whole school would love me!"

She felt tears welling up in her throat as the stream of words ebbed away. She started to loosen her grip on the emerald. Then suddenly she saw a startling image behind her closed eyes.

It looked like an enormous golden ball, almost transparent like a bubble, floating gently down out of the clear blue sky. But the instant it touched the ground, the golden bubble evaporated. In its place appeared a beautiful young girl, dressed in a pale green gown trimmed in silver-and-gold braid. She looked to Ezzie like some kind of fairy princess. Her crown and parts of her dress were studded with gleaming, bright jewels. The only one Ezzie could make out for certain was a single, large, brilliant green emerald that hung on a chain about her throat.

Ezzie almost gasped out loud. Never in her daydreams had she imagined anything so vividly before.

5

BEWARE OF
DOG!

THE SOUND OF a car horn startled Ezzie, and she opened her eyes. Without realizing it, she had circled the park and found herself standing across from the school parking lot again, just as Ms. Francis was pulling away in her little brown car. The teacher smiled and waved at her, and Ezzie waved back.

She remembered something that Ms. Francis often said: "With me, boys and girls, every morning is like a clean slate." Some of the kids used to giggle when she said that, but Ezzie knew that it meant that no matter what a person said or did, no matter how bad or stupid they were, as far as Ms. Francis was concerned, it would be forgotten the next day. You could start out all clean, just like the slate.

She felt the emerald in her hand. For a few moments, she'd forgotten all about it. She shoved it back into her pocket, clutching it tight in her fingers, and tried closing her eyes again to see if the beautiful image would come back. But the image seemed to have dissolved away completely. Even the memory of it made her feel lighter, and she broke into a skip as she headed home.

She turned the corner of Margaret and Willow streets, still skipping. When she got to her and Angela's hopscotch, she hopped right through it without even slowing down. As she approached the Di Cecco's, she saw Baby Nina playing in the front yard, surrounded by the short green picket fence that was just high enough to keep her from climbing over.

"Hi, Nina!" she called down the street to the little girl, who laughed and waved in response.

Suddenly she stopped and looked around. Something was wrong. What was it? She realized she was standing in front of the BEWARE OF DOG sign. But the front yard was empty. The dog was nowhere to be seen. Great, Ezzie thought. Peace and quiet. No snarling and barking as she passed the fence.

Then she noticed the gate was open. The wire that held it shut was dangling off one end. It looked like it had been pulled and snapped.

As she passed the next house she heard a rustling behind a large bush. Then she looked over onto the lawn and saw the dog standing right there, gnawing on a stick.

The dog's head snapped up. He looked right at Ezzie. At first she stood frozen to the spot. Then she remembered something someone had told her once: Never stare at a dog, especially a mean one. And never run away. Just turn around and walk away, slowly. Act like you don't even see it.

Ezzie quietly turned and started walking back up the street. She could feel the dog's gaze still fixed upon her, and she fought an urge to bolt and run. Slow, slow, she told herself.

Carefully, she turned around, and saw the dog walking down the street. Relieved, she hung back behind a bush, waiting till he got farther away before she started toward the DiCecco's.

Then something gripped her insides. Baby Nina! What if ... ? She ran back out to the sidewalk. The dog had stopped right by the DiCecco's fence, and was looking intently into the yard. There was Baby Nina, staring back at the dog, pointing and laughing.

Ezzie looked around. There was no one in sight. What should she do?

She looked up the street again. The dog was bounding over the picket fence, heading straight for the baby! Ezzie ran back up the street, yelling "Hey!" and jumped over the fence after him.

She saw Mrs. DiCecco race out the front door, screaming. The dog ran toward Nina, but before he could get to her, Ezzie leapt forward and grabbed on to the rope attached to his collar.

The dog's head snapped back sharply with the force of Ezzie's pull, and he struggled against it, twisting his body and snarling fiercely. Ezzie didn't know how long she could hold on. The dog was so strong. It was taking every bit of strength she had just to keep pulling on the rope.

Then the dog turned on Ezzie herself, lunging at her in fury. He dug his teeth into Ezzie's elbow. She screamed in pain and terror. Blood began to ooze out where he broke through the skin.

Suddenly she saw a pair of dark, hairy arms grab the dog by the neck, while another pair of strong hands lifted her up. She turned and looked into the face of Mr. DiCecco, who held her tightly, clutching her bleeding elbow. His nephew, Frank, grabbed the rope and dragged the snarling dog into the backyard. Ezzie watched him tie the rope tightly to one of the fence posts. Then he came back out front, slamming the backyard gate behind him.

"I'm calling the cops!" Frank shouted, bounding into the house.

It was then that Ezzie realized how frightened she was. Her body started to shake all over, and she let out big, heaving sobs. Mrs. DiCecco ran to her, still holding the crying Nina, and wrapped Ezzie's elbow with the tea towel she'd been carrying on her shoulder. Ezzie felt the strong arms of Mr. DiCecco around her, while from below her, she could hear Angela murmuring comforting words.

"What a brave girl! She save the baby!" cried Mrs. DiCecco.

"Little Ezzie," Mr. DiCecco said, patting her head as she sobbed. "You're such a strong little girl. You don't know how strong you are!"

6

A PERSON OF SOME IMPORTANCE

NEXT MORNING Ezzie still couldn't quite believe that it hadn't all been a dream.

"Look, Ezzie, look!" Anna screeched, racing toward her, carrying the morning paper as she walked into the kitchen.

"Girl, 8, saves baby from vicious dog" read the headline. Beneath it was a large picture of squirming Baby Nina, a beaming Mrs. DiCecco, and a somewhat stunned-looking Ezzie, holding up her bandaged elbow. "Story on page 5" read the caption underneath.

Ezzie turned to page 5. So it really had happened! Nina. The dog. The policemen. Going to the hospital to get her elbow bandaged. The reporters and TV cameras. All the neighbours cheering as she emerged from the car coming home.

Just then her mom came in through the door, carrying a stack of newspapers.

"I bought a whole bunch," she said. "For your grandparents and the other relatives, and people at the office. Oh, and Ezzie? I'll put one up here on top of the fridge, to send to your dad. Okay?"

Ezzie's stomach was so jumpy she could hardly eat any breakfast. Her mom and Anna were the same way. They all kept recounting the events of the previous day, squealing with excitement and interrupting each other with little anecdotes. Finally, Ezzie's mom put the half-full bowls of cereal in the sink, and they all started getting ready to leave.

The phone rang. Ezzie raced to get it.

"Hello?"

"Is that the famous girl-hero, Ezzie Phelan?"

"Daddy!"

"I just got back from jogging, picked up the paper on the front step, and pow! I could hardly believe my eyes. Right there on the front of the national edition!"

Breathlessly, Ezzie began telling him everything that had happened. After a couple of minutes her mom put Anna on the phone for a quick hello, then quietly kissed Ezzie on the forehead and left with Anna.

Ezzie's dad asked question after question, until finally Ezzie told him the whole story, some things twice over. Ezzie asked about Charlotte Rose, and they talked about her and other things. Finally there was a pause in the conversation.

"Dad? I was wondering if you got my valentine."

"Oh, honey! Sure I did. I kept meaning to send you kids a valentine, but I've been swamped at work."

"Yeah. I figured you were busy with the

baby and everything."

"You're not upset with me, Ezzie. Are you?"

Ezzie took a deep breath. "Well, I was. Kind of."

For a few seconds her dad didn't say anything.

"I'm sorry, honey. I forgot how much that stuff means to you. I'll try to do better from now on. Really I will. Ezzie?"

"Yeah?"

"I'm so proud of you I could burst."

Finally they said goodbye. Ezzie left the house and felt herself almost literally flying up the street, past the big bush, past the wired gate, past the BEWARE OF DOG sign. It felt weird, seeing the empty front yard, knowing the dog wouldn't be there any more. It gave her the creeps a bit to think they might — how did her mother say it? — "put down" the dog. But Mr. DiCecco said it wasn't to punish the dog, but to make sure it couldn't hurt anyone else ever again.

"Anyway," he told her, "there are no bad dogs, only bad people. The way he treated that poor animal, no wonder it turned out so mean."

When she got to school, she walked through the gate to the playground and noticed Shay pointing at her and talking to a bunch of other Grade 7 girls.

"Hey, Ezzie. Saw your picture in the paper this morning!"

Ezzie's face flushed. She was embarrassed, but proud, too. Several boys, including Jake, looked up at the mention of the newspaper.

"Whose picture was in the paper?"

"Ezzie's? How come?"

"She's the big hero," said Shay. "She saved a little baby from a big mean dog."

"Come on," said Jake.

"Really," said Shay. "She held it down until the mother grabbed the baby away from it."

"Sheesh," said Jake. "How'd you do that?"

Ezzie just shrugged. Then she felt a hand on her back.

"Nice going, Ez," said Josh.

Suddenly Sarah and Mai came running up from behind her, laughing and screaming. She'd already talked to both of them last night on the phone. Soon she was surrounded by a large group of Grade 3 girls, jumping, screeching, giggling.

When the bell rang, everyone filed into Ms. Francis' room. The teacher immediately got up from her desk and walked into the centre of the room.

"Good morning, class," she said. "It seems we have a person of some importance with us this morning." She held up the newspaper with the huge photo of Ezzie, Mrs. DiCecco and Baby Nina.

Ms. Francis read aloud: "An eight-year-old Margaret Street girl rescued a baby from serious harm yesterday afternoon. Esme Phelan" — Ms. Francis looked up briefly and nodded in Ezzie's direction — "prevented the dog from attacking nineteen-month-old Nina DiCecco, by holding on to its leash until the baby's relatives were able to restrain the dog."

Ms. Francis closed the newspaper. The room buzzed with a mixture of whistles, whispers, rustling movements.

"There's more, but I'm going to leave the article up here on the board as one of today's reading assignments. Now what shall we do, class, to acknowledge Esme's courage and quick thinking?"

The room burst into fierce applause. Ezzie felt her face going red and tried to cover it with her hands, but that only seemed to make them laugh and clap even louder. As she looked through the cracks between her fingers, she could see Mai, Sarah, Melodie, even Lisa, cheering fiercely, and Ms. Francis vigorously applauding. Josh was waving his arms over his head, beaming at her, and Jake was banging the top of his desk with his fist, yelling, "All right! All right!"

When she thought she wouldn't be able to stand it one second longer, Ms. Francis abruptly stopped clapping. The cheering and applause quickly died down.

"Let's get to work," the teacher said briskly, walking over to the blackboard.

At recess that morning a large group of kids clustered around Ezzie again, asking her question after question.

"What kind of dog was it?"

"Was there blood?"

"Weren't you scared?"

"My dad says people get superhuman strength when they're in real danger," said one of the boys.

"Yeah!" Jake piped up. "Like that guy whose kid was stuck under a car? He lifted the whole thing up all by himself!"

"Go on!"

"No kidding!"

"Was it like that, Ezzie?" asked Mai.

Ezzie suddenly remembered her emerald. She fished around and found it tucked into a corner of her pocket.

"I don't know," she said. "Maybe."

7

NOT QUITE
BACK TO
NORMAL

FOR A FEW DAYS it was like Ezzie's whole life was turned topsy-turvy. Another newspaper called, and someone from the radio wanted to interview her. At recess, kids still clustered around her, and some of the little kids even acted out what had happened, taking the parts of the dog, Baby Nina, and Ezzie herself.

Then, after a week or so, Ezzie noticed that the newspaper clippings on the kitchen table had finally all gotten mailed off to the relatives, and she knew it was all over. She felt a little sorry, but she was also glad that her life had gotten back to normal. It had been almost too much excitement.

Finally, one day, it all started again. At afternoon recess.

She was playing horses with Mai and Sarah, when she saw Jake cup his hands over his mouth and bellow "Hippo! Hippo!" as she ran past. At first, like always, she tried to pretend she didn't hear him. Suddenly something snapped inside her.

She turned and walked right up to Jake, looking him straight in the eye.

"I'm sick and tired of you doing that, Jake! Cut it out!"

He laughed nervously.

"C'mon! I was just kidding around."

Sarah ran over, beside Ezzie, and Mai came up behind them.

"How would you feel if someone made fun of you that way?" Ezzie yelled at Jake.

"You wouldn't think it was very funny!" Mai added.

By now the whole playground was watching, including Ms. Francis, who was on supervision duty.

"Okay, okay! Sorry!" Jake finally said sheepishly.

The bell rang. As the kids streamed into the building, Ezzie saw Josh making his way through the throng. Without saying a word, he came up and started walking beside her.

As she walked through the big doors flanked by her friends, Ezzie reached into her pocket and felt the tiny, smooth columns of the emerald, which she now always carried with her. She thought of that day, and Mr. DiCecco saying: "Little Ezzie, you don't know how strong you are."

I do now, she thought.

THE END